Hey
Diddle Diddle

Eve Bunting

Illustrated by Mary Ann Fraser

BOYDS MILLS PRESS
HONESDALE, PENNSYLVANIA

Boyds Mills Press, Inc.
815 Church Street
Honesdale, Pennsylvania 18431
Printed in the United States of America

ISBN: 978-1-59078-768-7

Library of Congress Control Number: 2010929543

First edition
The text of this book is set in 20-point Life Light.
The illustrations are done in acrylic.

10 9 8 7 6 5 4 3 2 1

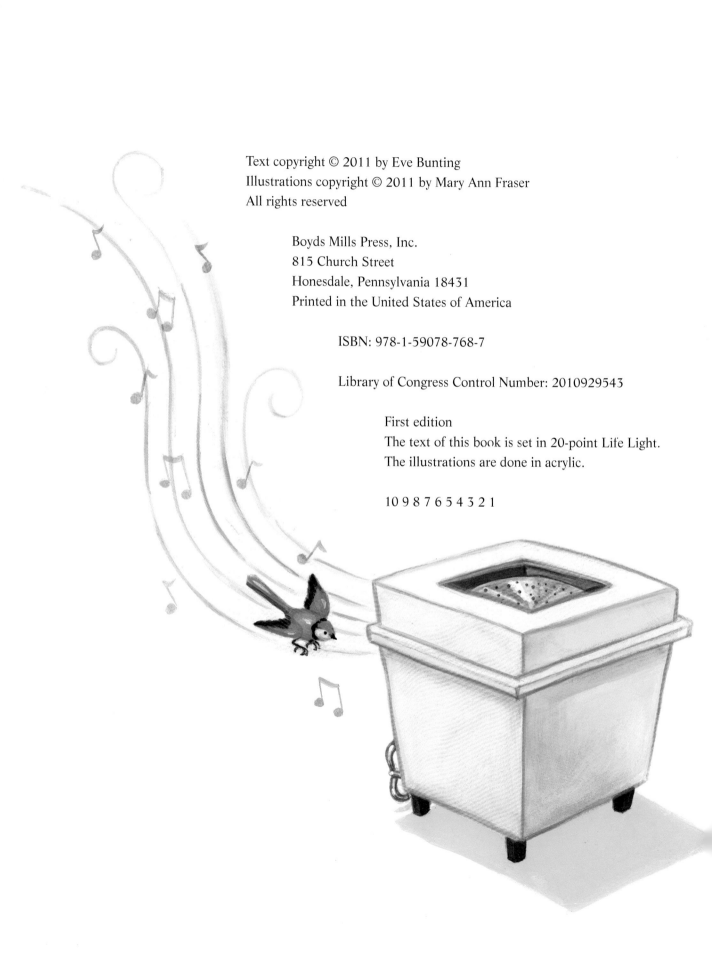

For Keelin Taylor Bunting
    —E.B.

To Lori Cook
    —M.A.F.

Hey diddle diddle, the cat plays the fiddle,

the cow plays the silver trombone.

Hey diddle dum, the whale bangs the drum,

the seal's on the big saxophone.

Hey diddle dar,
the horse strums guitar,

the pig plays piano with grace.

Hey diddle dumpet,
the camel blows trumpet,

the elephant's awesome on bass.

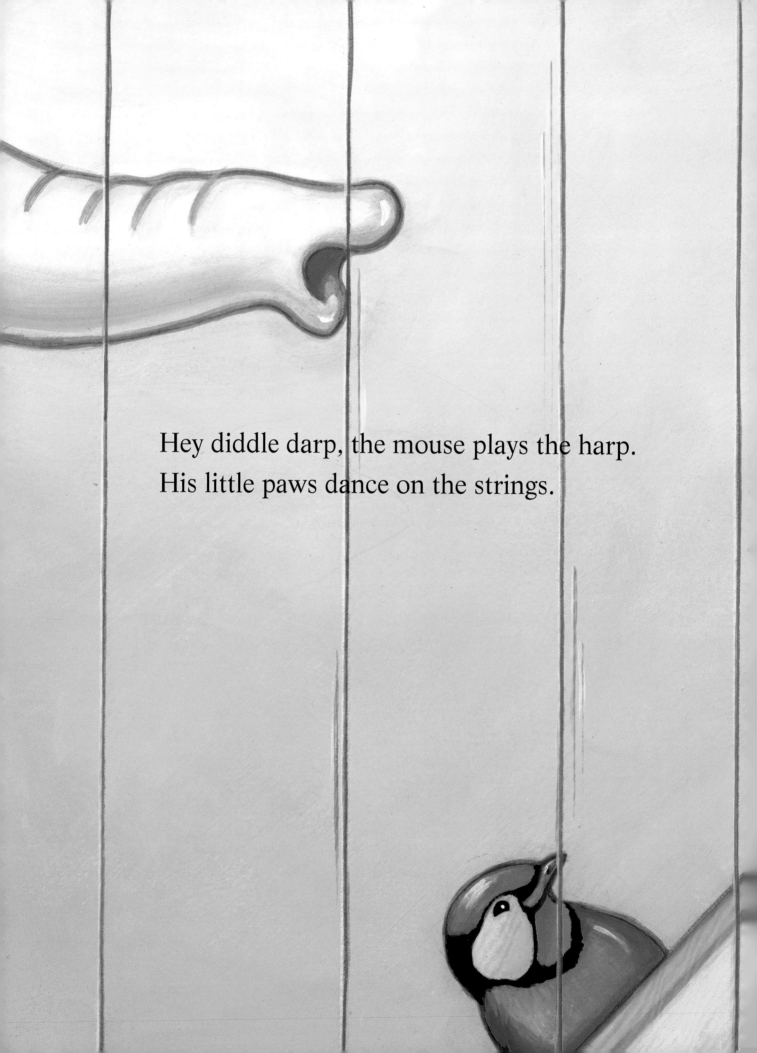

Hey diddle darp, the mouse plays the harp.
His little paws dance on the strings.

The lion blows flute
with a tootldy toot,

the rhino is starting to sing.

Hey diddle deddy, is everyone ready?
The dog strokes his spotted bow tie.
He's dapper and grand as he faces the band,
holding his baton up high.

So, hey diddle dusic, for marvelous music
there's only one thing left to do.

Hey diddle dee, just wind up the key.

Let the music box band play for you.